W9-CBE-199

# Double Trouble

## ALL ABOUT COLORS

# Written by Kirsten Hall
# Illustrated by Bev Luedecke

## children's press®

**A Division of Scholastic Inc.**
New York  Toronto  London  Auckland  Sydney
Mexico City  New Delhi  Hong Kong
Danbury, Connecticut

## About the Author

Kirsten Hall, formerly an early-childhood teacher,
is a children's book editor in New York City. She has been
writing books for children since she was thirteen years old
and now has over sixty titles in print.

## About the Illustrator

Bev Luedecke enjoys life and nature in Colorado.
Her sparkling personality and artistic flair are reflected in her
creation of Beastieville, a world filled with lovable Beasties
that are sure to delight children of all ages.

Library of Congress Cataloging-in-Publication Data

Hall, Kirsten.
  Double trouble : all about colors / written by Kirsten Hall ;
illustrated by Bev Luedecke.
     p. cm.
Summary: Toggles paints such lifelike portraits of her friends, Slider
mistakes the pictures for real Beasties.
  ISBN 0-516-22892-7 (lib.bdg.) 0-516-24653-4 (pbk.)
  [1. Painting–Fiction. 2. Friendship–Fiction. 3. Stories in rhyme.]
I. Luedecke, Bev, ill. II. Title.
  PZ8.3.H146Do 2003
  [E]–dc21
                        2003001586

1 2 3 4 5 6 7 8 9 10 R 12 11 10 09 08 07 06 05 04 03

# A NOTE TO PARENTS AND TEACHERS

Welcome to the world of the Beasties, where learning is FUN. In each of the charming stories in this series, the Beasties deal with character traits that every child can identify with. Each story reinforces appropriate concept skills for kindergartners and first graders, while simultaneously encouraging problem-solving skills. Following are just a few of the ways that you can help children get the most from this delightful series.

### Stories to be read and enjoyed

Encourage children to read the stories aloud. The rhyming verses make them fun to read. Then ask them to think about alternate solutions to some of the problems that the Beasties have faced or to imagine alternative endings. Invite children to think about what they would have done if they were in the story and to recall similar things that have happened to them.

### Activities reinforce the learning experience

The activities at the end of the books offer a way for children to put their new skills to work. They complement the story and are designed to help children develop specific skills and build confidence. Use these activities to reinforce skills. But don't stop there. Encourage children to find ways to build on these skills during the course of the day.

### Learning opportunities are everywhere

Use this book as a starting point for talking about how we use reading skills or math or social studies concepts in everyday life. When we search for a phone number in the telephone book and scan names in alphabetical order or check a list, we are using reading skills. When we keep score at a baseball game or divide a class into even-numbered teams, we are using math.

The more you can help children see that the skills they are learning in school really do have a place in everyday life, the more they will think of learning as something that is part of their lives, not as a chore to be borne. Plus you will be sending the important message that learning is fun.

Madeline Boskey Olsen, Ph.D.
Developmental Psychologist

Bee-Bop

Puddles

Slider

Wilbur

Pip & Zip

Flippet

Pooky

Mr. Rigby

Smudge

We're the Beasties

Toggles

Toggles looks outside her window.
It is raining. It is gray.

Toggles cannot see her friends.
There is too much rain to play.

Toggles looks around her room.
She does not know what to do.

Then she sees her jars of paints.
Then she sees her brushes, too!

"I will paint myself!" thinks Toggles.
She starts painting. It looks great.

"I must let this picture dry now.
I will paint more while I wait!"

Toggles starts by painting Puddles.
How will she paint her green fur?

She will mix the blue and yellow.
There! Now that looks just like her!

Next, she will paint Mr. Rigby.
He has on a nice blue tie.

Smudge is red and he is tall.
Toggles has to reach up high.

All the wet paint needs to dry now.
Toggles likes what she has done.

"What a painting! It is perfect!
Painting this was so much fun!"

The rain has stopped. The sun is out.
Outside, Slider passes by.

"Everyone is here with Toggles!
No one told me. Why, oh why?"

Slider sadly slides away.
"Smudge! What are you doing here?